THIS WALKER BOOK BELONGS TO:

_____

_____

_____

First published 1996 by Walker Books Ltd
87 Vauxhall Walk, London SE11 5HJ

This edition published 2007

2 4 6 8 10 9 7 5 3 1

Text © 1996 Michael Rosen
Illustrations © 1996 Blackbird Design Pty.

The moral rights of the author and illustrator have been asserted.

This book has been typeset in Bob Graham font.

Printed in China

British Library Cataloguing in Publication Data:
a catalogue record for this book is available from the British Library.

ISBN: 978-1-4063-0564-7

www.walkerbooks.co.uk

This Is Our House

MICHAEL ROSEN   BOB GRAHAM

WALKER BOOKS

AND SUBSIDIARIES

LONDON • BOSTON • SYDNEY • AUCKLAND

George was in the house.

"This house is mine and no one else is coming in," George said.

"It's not your house, George," said Lindy.

"It belongs to everybody."

"No it doesn't," said George.
"This house is all for me!"

Lindy and Marly went
for a walk over to
the swings.

"It's not George's house,
is it?" said Lindy.
"Of course it isn't," said Marly.

Lindy and Marly looked
through the window.
"It's not your house George,
and we're coming in."

"Oh, no you're not,"
said George.
"This house isn't for girls."

Freddie was walking past with his Rabbity.
"I've come to put Rabbity to bed," said Freddie.

"You can't," said George.

"This house isn't for small people like you."

Freddie took Rabbity for a ride in the car.

Charlene and Marlene mended the front wheel.

"George won't let me and Rabbity in the house," said Freddie.

Charlene and Marlene, Freddie and Rabbity
headed straight for the house.

"Stop right there," said George.

"We're coming in to mend the fridge,"
said Charlene and Marlene.

"Oh, no you're not," said George.
"This house isn't for twins."

Luther's jumbo jet landed
in the house.
He went to fetch it.
"Where do you think
you're going?" said George.

"Flight 505 has crashed,"
said Luther. "And I'm
coming in for the rescue.
Fire! Fire! Ee-ah-ee-
ah-ee-ah!"

"You're not coming in here,"
said George.

Luther radioed for help. "Calling Dr Sophie. Calling Dr Sophie."

"Can I help you?" said Sophie.

"We can't get at the plane, Doctor," said Luther.

"Leave it to me," said Sophie.

Sophie and Luther pushed past the crowds.

"Make way for the doctor," said Luther.

"We're coming in," said Sophie.

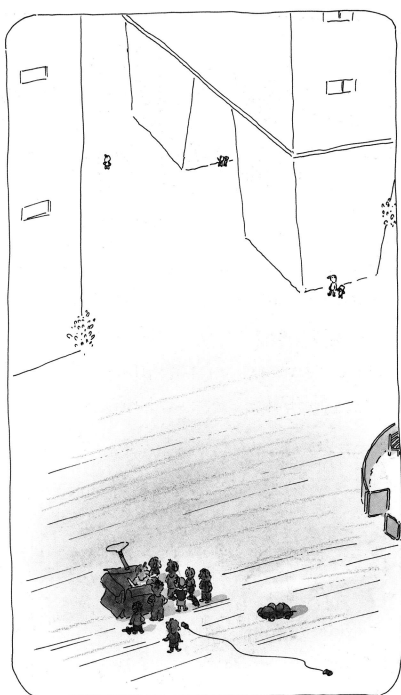

"Oh, no you're not," said George.
"This house isn't for people
with glasses."

Rasheda had a plan. "I'm going to tunnel in."
She poked her head under the house.
"Go away," said George. "This is my house."
"Well, this is my tunnel," said Rasheda.

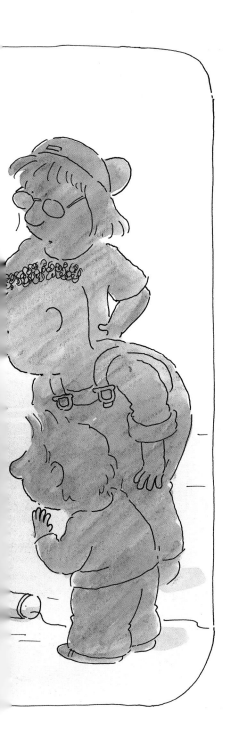

"Well, tunnel somewhere else," said
George. "This house isn't for
people who like tunnels."

It was getting quite noisy around the house now. And hot. And George wanted to go to the toilet.

"I'm going to leave my house now," said George. "AND NO ONE CAN GO IN IT WHEN I'M GONE."

George went to the toilet.

Lindy, Marly, Freddie, Rabbity, Marlene,
Charlene, Luther, Sophie and Rasheda went
straight into the house.

George came back.

There was no room for George.

"This house isn't for people with red hair," said Charlene.

George began to shout.

George began to cry.

George began to stamp his
feet and kick the wall.

Then he stopped.
He looked.

"This house IS for people with red hair..." said George. "And for girls and small people and twins and people who wear glasses and like tunnels!"

"Because..." shouted Lindy, Marly, Freddie, Marlene, Charlene, Luther, Sophie and Rasheda—

"THIS HOUSE IS FOR **EVERYONE!**"

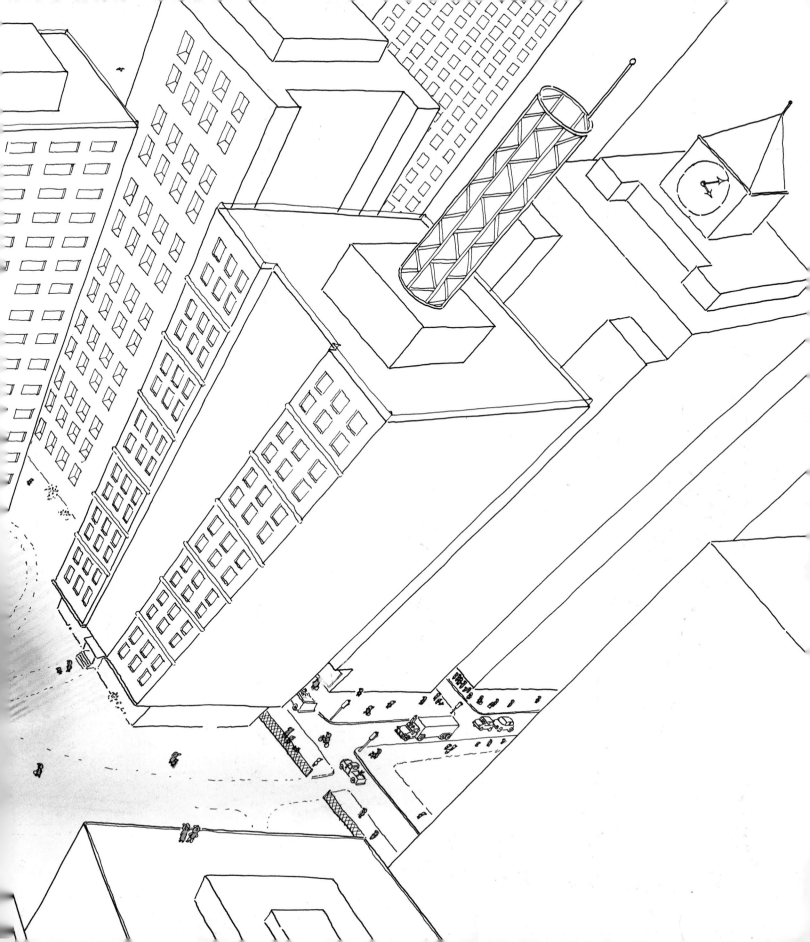

WALKER BOOKS is the world's leading
independent publisher of children's books.
Working with the best authors and illustrators
we create books for all ages, from babies
to teenagers – books your child will
grow up with and always remember. So…

FOR THE BEST CHILDREN'S BOOKS,
LOOK FOR THE BEAR